There Is a TRIBE *of* KIDS

LANE SMITH

TWO HOOTS

For Jane Enlow

First published in the USA 2016 by Roaring Brook Press
This edition published in the UK 2016 by Two Hoots
an imprint of Pan Macmillan
20 New Wharf Road, London N1 9RR
Associated companies throughout the world
www.panmacmillan.com
ISBN 978-1-5098-1288-2

Book design by Molly Leach

9 8 7 6 5 4 3 2 1
A CIP catalogue record for this book is available from the British Library.
Printed in China

The illustrations in this book were painted in oils and sprayed with an acrylic varnish to create various mottled textures. Also used were coloured pencils, graphite, traditional cut and paste, and digital cut and paste.

www.twohootsbooks.com

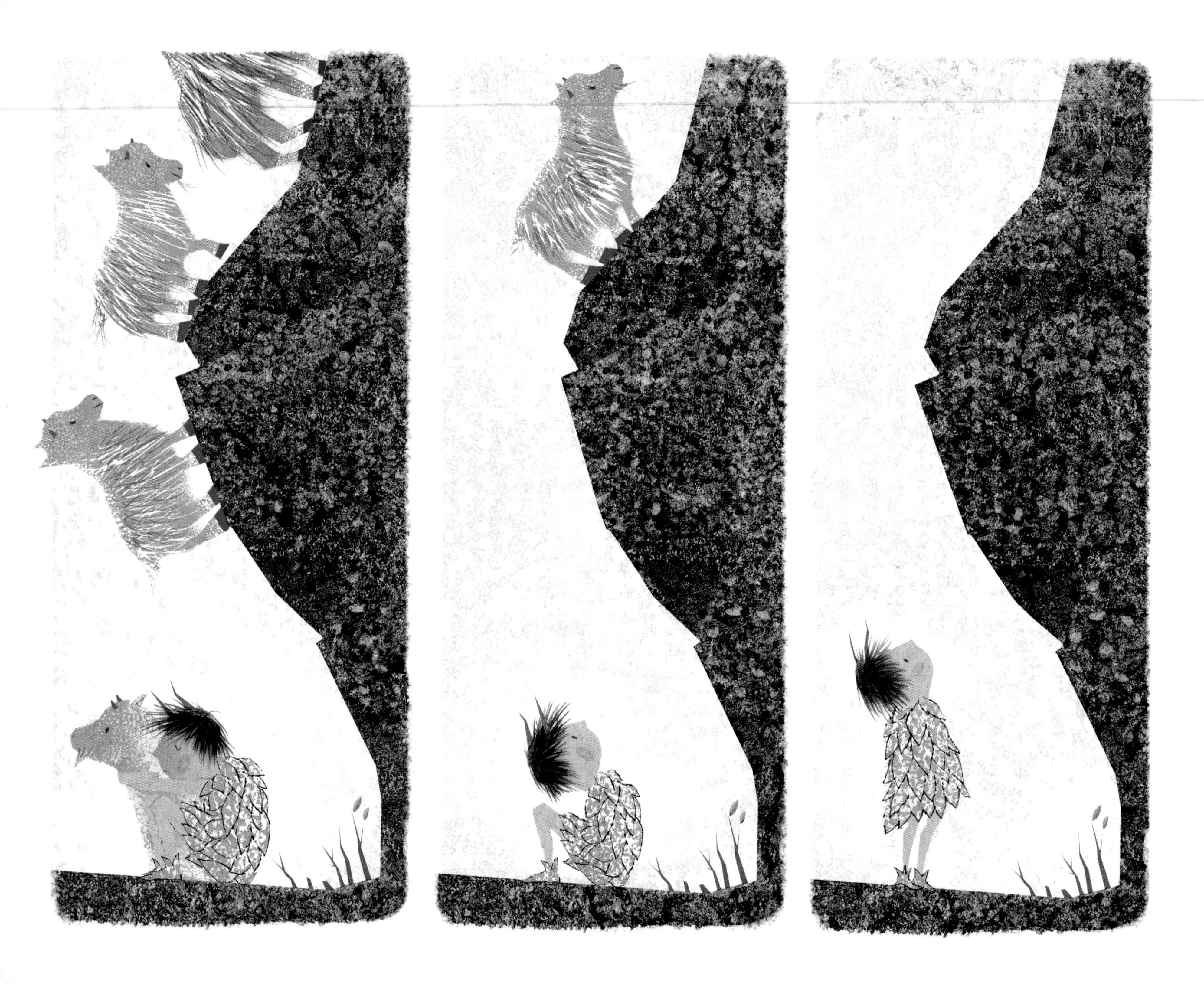

There was a TRIBE *of* KIDS.

There was a COLONY *of* PENGUINS.

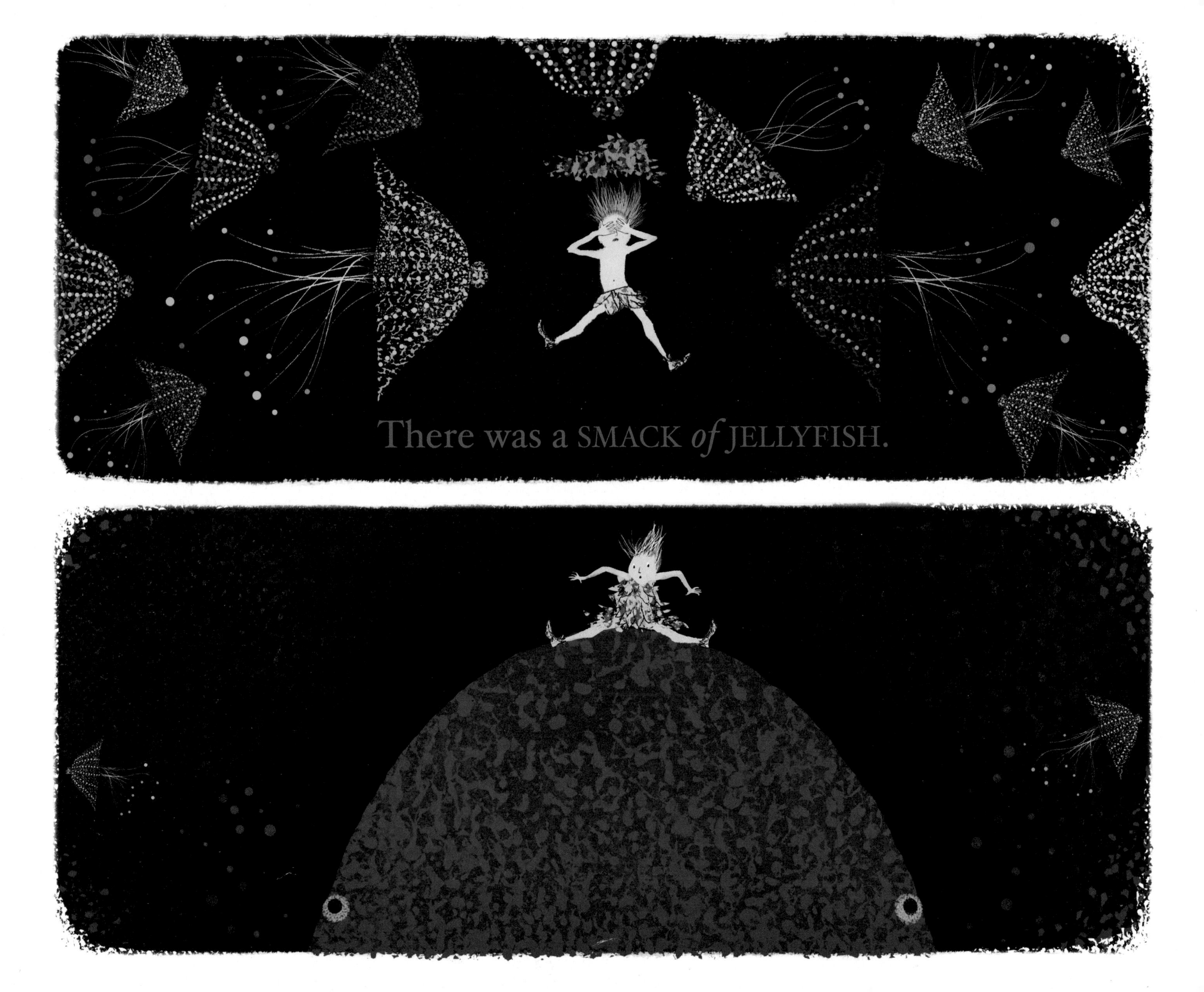
There was a SMACK *of* JELLYFISH.

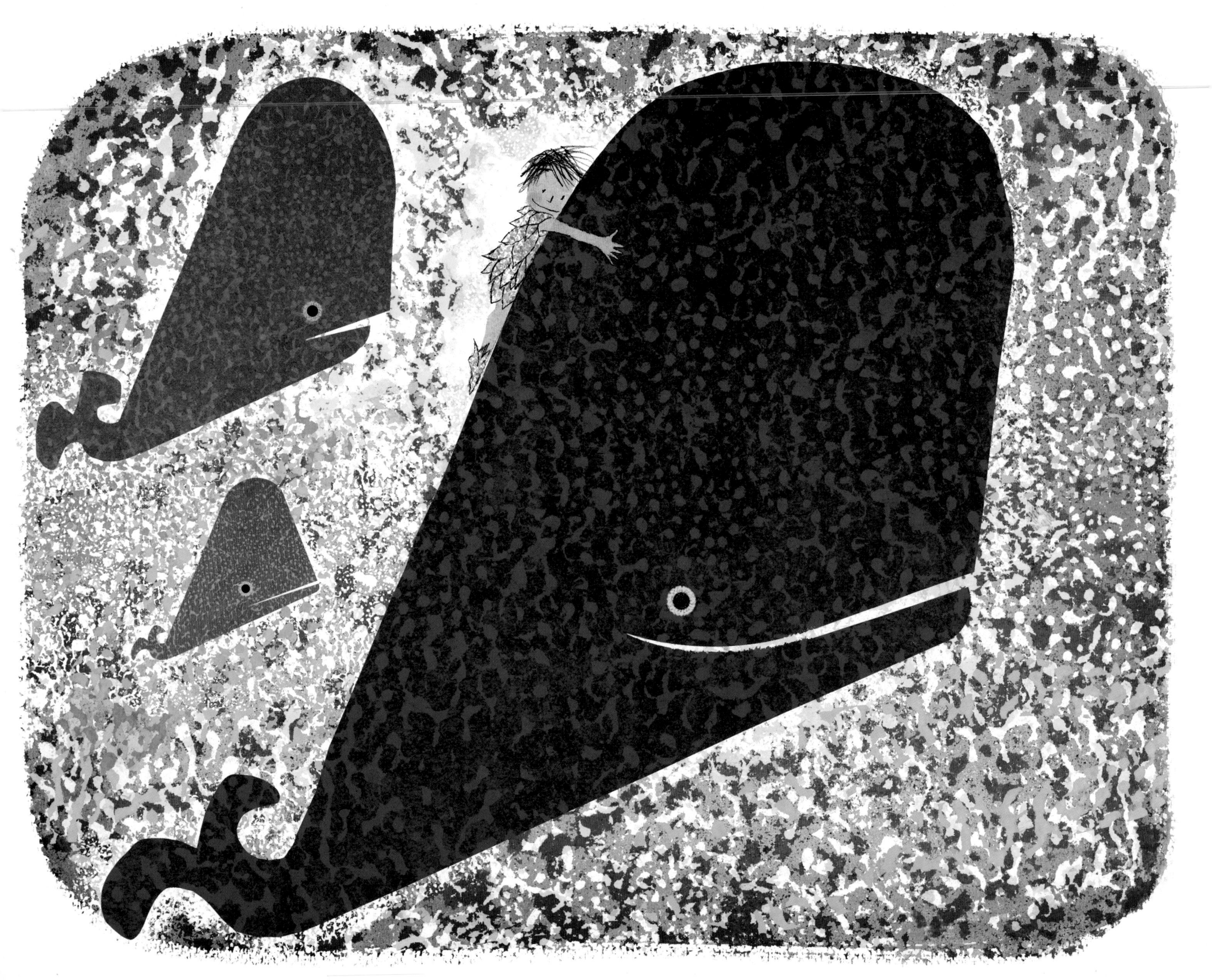

There was
a POD
of WHALES.

There was an
UNKINDNESS *of* RAVENS.

There was a FORMATION *of* ROCKS.

There was a

PILE *of* RUBBLE.

There was a GROWTH *of* PLANTS.

There was a

PARADE *of* ELEPHANTS.

There was a TROOP *of* MONKEYS.

There was a CRASH *of* RHINOS.

There was a BAND *of* GORILLAS.

There was a TURN *of* TURTLES.

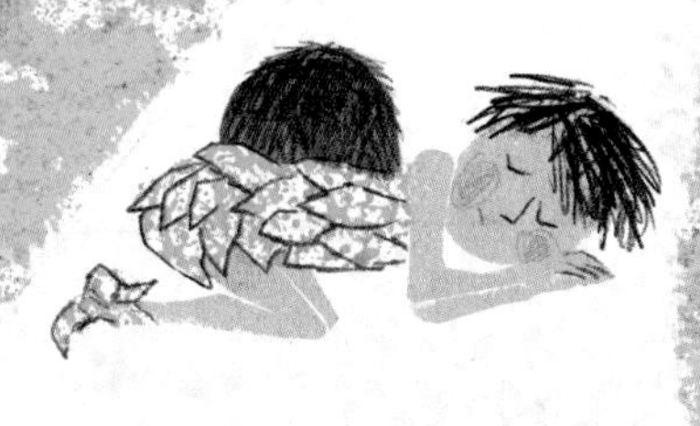

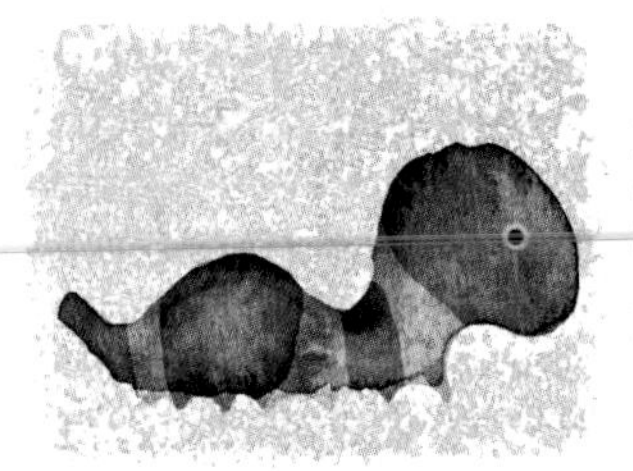

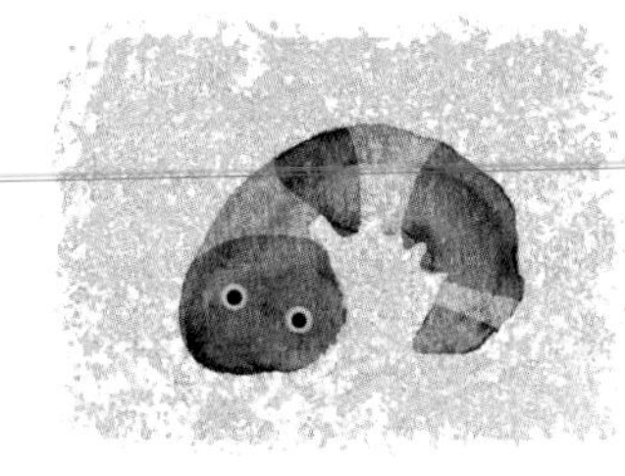

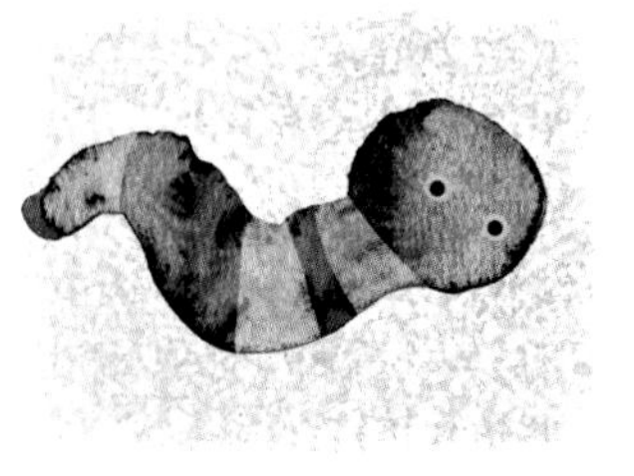

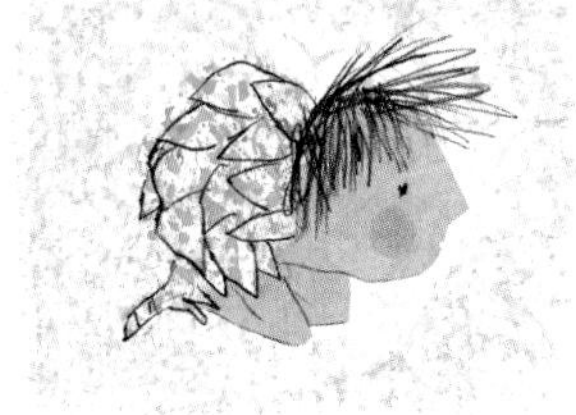

There was an ARMY *of* CATERPILLARS.

There was a FLIGHT
of BUTTERFLIES.

There was a SPRINKLE
of FIREFLIES.

There was a FAMILY *of* STARS.

There was an OCEAN *of* BLUE.

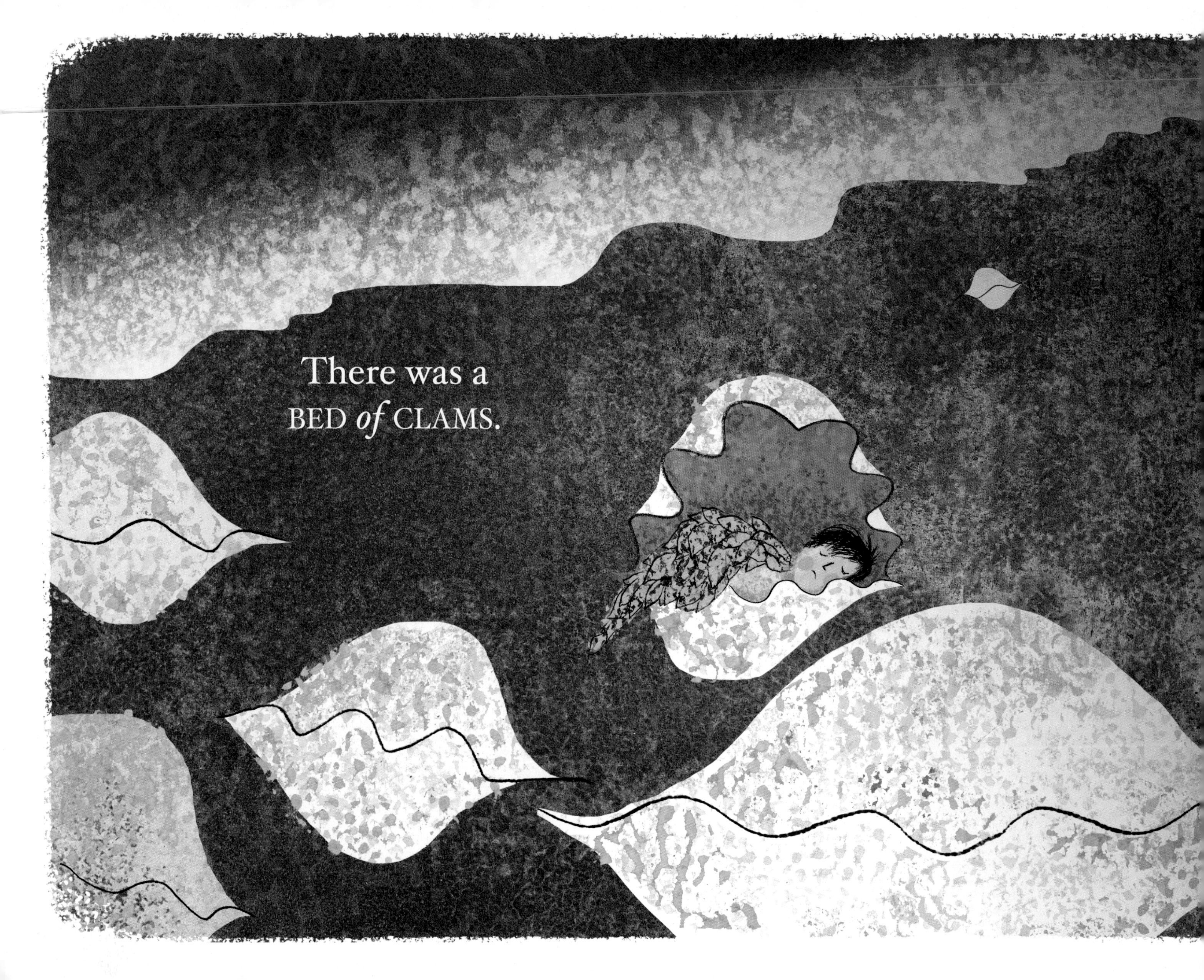

There was a
BED *of* CLAMS.

There was a NIGHT *of* DREAMS.

There was a
TRAIL *of* SHELLS.

There was . . .

a TRIBE *of* KIDS.

There is a

TRIBE *of* KIDS.